PARANORMAL ROMANCE

I0520114

THE
WIZARD CASEY'S
COVEN

THE INNKEEPER'S WIZARD BOOK 2

JACK RYDER

About the Publisher

4Fun Publishing, a member of **BLVNP Incorporated**, 340 S. Lemon #6200, Walnut CA 91789, info@blvnp.com / legal@blvnp.com
NOTE: Due to the highly emotional reaction of some people to works of erotic fiction, any email sent to the above address that contains foul language or religious references is automatically deleted by our anti-spam software and will not be seen. All other communications are welcome.

DISCLAIMER

Please don't be stupid and kill yourself. This book is a work of FICTION. Do not try any new sexual practice that you find in this book. It is fiction and not to be confused with reality. Neither the author nor the publisher or its associates assume any responsibility for any loss, injury, death or legal consequences resulting from acting on the contents in this book. Every character in this book is over 18 years of age. The author's opinions are not to be construed as the opinions of the publisher. The material in this book is for entertainment purposes ONLY. Enjoy.

The Innkeeper's Wizard Book 2

The Wizard Casey's Coven

Paranormal Romance

By: Jack Ryder

© Jack Ryder 2014
ISBN: 978-1-62761-692-8

Chapter One

This is a journey that Casey had never expected. It has been filled with self-discovery, deep passionate love and a sexual freedom that he had never thought could exist. Once, he was convinced that he would live out his days alone. He had given up hope of ever having a lasting relationship with any woman. He had learned to satisfy his sexual needs with hookers and his fantasizes about his boss Rosalind. Little did he know that his fantasizes were tame compared to the reality of his new existence.

Fate had stepped in very abruptly and unexpectedly. It was a supposed to be a routine insurance investigation in a sleepy ski resort town in the higher elevations of Utah. But the moment that Casey met Roni, owner of Veronica's Bed and Breakfast, everything had changed and his life would never be the same. It would never be normal ever again. He would never again be alone.

~~oOo~~

Tomorrow it will be Thanksgiving. Exactly one year from that first night that Veronica invited Rosalind into our bed. One year since the three of us became mated for life. One year since I had filled Rosalind's belly with my child, one year since the three of us discovered a world that none of us could ever have guessed could be possible.

Early in the pregnancy, we discovered that because of the supernatural physical connection between us that Veronica seemed to experience all of the same pregnancy sensations along with Roz. Later, when Rosalind began to lactate, Veronica did too. It was amazing to watch the both of them as they experienced the entire pregnancy together.

Although Rosalind was the one physically carrying Daxx inside, he became physically and supernaturally bound to them both. He, in effect, had two mothers from the moment of his conception. During the process of the pregnancy, Roz and Roni became so close with each other and so bonded, that they became like twins of one another.

By the time that Rosalind went into labor and was ready to give birth, they had already learned how to join their powers together to block out any pain or discomfort. Because of this, Roz was able to have an effortless and relatively pain free delivery. From the moment that Daxx was born he took favor to both of them as his mother and was able to nurse from each of them effortlessly. He did, in fact, have two mothers.

The last trimester of the pregnancy had been a little difficult on me though. My sex life had dwindled considerably as they both went through the physical and emotional changes of the pregnancy. I was elated to see how wonderfully close and bonded that they were becoming. But, at times, I was beginning to feel a little left out. I was feeling like they had both forgotten that they once had both been absolutely crazy about me.

I made it a point to block out my misery from them. I kept my mind busy with preparations to the house for our new addition. I spent many hours each day reading and studying books about Wizardry. Pouring through books about spells and rituals. Practicing and learning my new skills.

It was a slow process even though I seemed to effortlessly grasp each new lesson of interest and usually could perfect the skill by the second or third attempt. But there were mistakes and blunders along the way too. I had read that Wizards often use a wand to cast their spell or to create any effect that they desired. In my ignorance, I had used an ordinary tree branch on my first attempt. It exploded in my hand and had blown a three foot hole in the ground at my feet.

During those last 90 days of the pregnancy Roz and Roni became exceptionally close to one another. Once their breasts were lactating, they found that they could relieve the fullness and discomfort by breast feeding each other. This intimacy cemented the very fierce sexual bond and attraction that they had already enjoyed since the day they met. They would be lifelong lovers for the rest of their lives.

I did not go completely without sex during this period. Each afternoon I would help them with the process of extracting the milk from their breasts. Although we often used breast pumps so we could practice bottling it, I also took the opportunity each day to suckle some from each of their breasts. I found that I really enjoyed the taste of their ambrosia.

While I was sucking on the breasts of one of them, the other one would suck me off. It was the most pleasurable part of my day during those last 90 days. I sorely missed our usually very torrid sex life. But I knew that they were doing their best to keep me satisfied.

It was a Tuesday afternoon the first time it happened. I had spent the entire morning out back studying and practicing Chants and Spells with a good amount of success. I had also spent much of that time grumbling to myself about my increasing lack of sexual attention. Last Friday had been the last time and they had both seemed very distracted and uninterested. I had fallen asleep feeling like they no longer needed me since they had each other.

"Why don't you join us today for the afternoon *BoobieFest*." This was the cute little name they had come up with for their afternoon breast feeding time together. I felt a smile appearing on my face. "We would love to share that intimacy with you, Daddy." That was their newest term of endearment for me. They had both started calling me that the day the Doctor called us to inform Rozalind that she was indeed pregnant.

I will never forget that first experience as Rosalind's milk let down as I began to suck on her breast. It was the warmest and sweetest cream I had ever tasted. As it flowed freely into my mouth, my prick had become equally engorged inside of my sweatpants. As I began to suck on her other breast, I felt the magnificent hot wetness of Veronica's mouth sliding all the way down my rigidness.

"I want some of Daddy's milk," I heard Roni's playful angelic voice in my head. It was the most incredible feeling. Sucking in the warm creamy milk from Roz while Roni's mouth slowly bobbed up and down on my throbbing cock. *"Give me your cream, Daddy...Give me your cream,"* Roni whispered into my brain.

As I edged closer and closer to my climax, I noticed that they were both diddling themselves and I could feel their orgasms approaching too. As I sucked greedily the last drops from Roz's breast, the added stimulation sent all three of us over the edge. The sensation of three climaxes all bursting and radiating through me simultaneously was spectacular. As I gushed my seed into Veronica's throat, they both convulsed and jerked and I could see the wetness of their orgasms glistening all over their thighs.

The Boobie Fest became our daily playtime for the next 90 days. Although it relieved much of the sexual tension inside of me, I still felt a bit left out. I felt like the intimacy I had once shared with both of them was now theirs alone. I was feeling pretty sorry for myself as the due date was just within a few days.

It was a quarter till midnight when Veronica crawled into bed with me. I had been sleeping alone for the last three months since they both had to get up so many times at night to use the toilet or relieve their milk flow. It felt almost foreign to me to have this soft warm body next to mine. At first, I thought I just having some stupid vivid erotic dream.

"We want to thank you for being so patient with us and understanding." Roni whispered it into my ear as her warm hand wrapped around my soft prick. *"We want to please you, Love."* It was the sound of Rosalind's sweet voice in my head. "Ooooh, God Yes," I gasped as Roni took my swelling prick into her mouth.

I could feel little warm drops of milk dripping down onto my thighs as her head slid up and down and brought me to full erection. It felt so sensuous as it began to drip down onto my belly and then ran down to my balls. "I want to feel you inside of me," Roni whispered as she crawled up and straddled my cock.

"Ooooh God...I've missed this." It was Roz's voice in my head as Veronica sat down onto my throbbing dick. *"Oooh Yes,* sweetie...*Oooh Yes,"* I could hear both of them moaning at the same time in my brain as Veronica very slowly rocked back and forth on my rigid prick. *"Tomorrow I'm going to have your child, Daddy...I'm going to give you a son."*

At that moment I felt the most overwhelming sensation of love flooding into me from the both of them. "We both love you so very much, Casey!" Roni said it very softly as she leaned forward and kissed me very passionately. As I began to suck the wonderful ambrosia from Roni's tits, she sped up her grinding on my throbbing pole.

As I felt the pressure building up towards my release, I could hear Rosalind's sweet voice in my head. *"I'm cumming with you, Daddy..I'm cumming too...I'm cumming too."* My back arched up off the bed as my climax blasted up into Veronica. "Yes Darling...Give it to me...Give it to me." Roni's voice was a low throaty moan as she began to jerk into her orgasm too. "We both wanted to do something special for you," Veronica informed me softly before she got up to go to bed. She kissed me on the cheek and told me to get a good night sleep. "Tomorrow's the big day!"

Chapter Two

As I said earlier, before I got off track with memories of the pregnancy, tomorrow will be Thanksgiving and also a very special anniversary for all three of us. It will always remain one of the most important anniversaries for us. The other equally important anniversary will occur every Christmas Eve Day. That was the day we were married. All three of us!

The wedding was magical in every essence of the word. Veronica happened to know of a Mage who has his coven of wives in the Southern corner of Utah near the Arches National Monument area. I soon discovered that Murphy the Wizard had four wives, eleven children and his wonderful property was once a Monastery.

The ceremony was held outside in the brisk December air under a huge 50 foot diameter Gazebo behind the main dwelling. The wives conjured up some star like lights in the night sky that appeared to be wedding bells and three interlaced hearts. They also conjured a wonderful Angelic Melody that could be heard softly throughout the ceremony.

"Are you all certain that this is what you desire?" Murphy asked after clearing his throat with a grunt. We assured him that we were all in agreement. "This is not like a normal matrimony," he advised. "Once this is done...there is no divorce!" He glanced over towards his four wives. "This is forever...there is no turning back!"

After we again assured him that all three of us wished to be joined together, he finally began the ritual. With all four of his wives chanting the same indistinguishable sentence over and over, he placed one hand on my head and had both of the girls each hold one of my hands.

With his other hand placed on his Master Book of Magic, he began to chant in a language that I had never heard before. Within moments, I started to feel warmth begin to radiate within me from my head down to my feet. As he continued to chant, I noticed that all three of us were beginning to glow. Like there was a great beacon within each of us that was being driven by his cadence. It got brighter and brighter as he continued.

By the time he completed his long ritualistic chant, that light had become so bright that it now appeared as if it were one huge ball of light. You could no longer distinguish any of the three of us as a single person. When he removed his hand from my head, the huge ball of light rose up out of us and exploded in a huge magnificent flash. The conjured stars above us realigned and now became one very large heart. Then we suddenly noticed that there was a second very tiny heart inside of the larger one.

"I see that one of you is with child," we observed softly. "Probably not you, though!" He gave me a sly little grin and a wink. "You know he will be...very gifted." His face became very serious.

"You need to take great care with him," he whispered it like a secret. "He will be very special!"

Before he had one of his wives escort us to the little cottage out back to start our honeymoon, Murphy again reminded us that we would be bonded together permanently. He also informed us that with this bond we could work together as "one mind and one will," as he put it. "You will be very strong together!" He told us.

The sex was unbelievable that first night in our wedding bed. From the moment that we were undressed and petting each other in the bed, that warm radiating sensation returned inside of all three of us. As we kissed and petted and fondled each other, that bright glowing light again began to glow inside too.

Veronica crawled up and mounted my rigidness while Rosalind

straddled my face. For the next twenty minutes they both slowly rocked back and forth in unison. It was thrilling to watch them kissing and fondling each other as they were grinding their sex into me. I could feel every sensation. I could feel the love, the greedy lust, the intense physical pleasure and the very deep feeling of joy. As the passions grew within each of us, that bright light grew stronger and stronger until it was once again one huge ball of light.

Rosalind was the first to climax. As she began to vibrate her pussy erupted and she sprayed her hot fluid all over my face and chest. Veronica followed her into climax almost instantly. As her body began to jerk, her pussy also began to spray all over my belly.

As my cock began to erupt deep inside of Veronica, the bright light again exploded into another magnificent flash. Except this time it was four flashes. One for each ejaculation deep into Veronica's womb. There was still a small residual glow within each of us as our bodies began to relax from our conjoined orgasm.

After they crawled down off of me, we laid there for quite some time with me cradled between them both. Each had an arm beneath the pillow under my head. Each had a leg draped over mine. Each had their breasts against my belly and their head on a shoulder. That was the first time that I felt it. We were one body, one mind and one spirit. It was the most extraordinary sensation I had ever felt. I fell asleep like that. The synchronized beating of our hearts, a soft sweet peaceful lullaby.

I felt them fondling one another in the shower when I awoke. I thought about joining them, but decided to it would be better to let them have their time alone to enjoy the new intimacy of being each other's wife. I could feel their appreciation and joy as I made the decision. I also felt the tidal wave of their passion as they both had their climaxes.

Within moments they were both on the bed with me still dripping wet. My dick was painfully rigid from the arousal of all the sexual energy they had created. It was thrilling to watch them touching and playing with each other as they took turns sucking on my prick. "You enjoy watching us, Huh?" it was Veronica's lovely transmitted voice. "Oh my god yes...Oh yes," I gasped my lust filled reply.

As she raised her head, Rosalind's mouth quickly took over licking and sucking as Roni slid her hand up underneath my ass. "Ooooh, My God Yes," I moaned as Roni slipped a finger deep into my rectum. I cannot describe how fantastic it felt as Rosalind finished sucking me off while

Veronica wiggled her finger up my ass and sucked a hickey onto my inner left thigh.

My legs suddenly became rigid and began to vibrate as I started to empty my load deep into Roz's throat. She managed to swallow most of the first two ejaculations. But the second two filled her mouth and began to gush out and ooze onto her tits. As I laid there quivering, I watched as Veronica licked all of my cum off Roz's tits. Then they shared a very long kiss as they swapped my semen back and forth between them.

Murphy was waiting for us in the huge kitchen area when we came into the monastery that morning. With a slight nod of his head, the four wives quickly left. "They will serve breakfast when we are done," he informed us. "But first, we need to talk." He had that serious look on his face again.

I noticed that he had that Master Book of Magic and Spells on the table. "Here...you are going to need this much more than I do," he told me softly as he slid it across the table to me. "There is trouble ahead for all of you." He said it quietly but with a grim determination. "It will take all three of you working together," he advised us. "She will be...very formidable...and..," he paused for a moment as if he dreaded the rest.

Then he clapped his hands twice and the four wives returned each carrying part of our meal with them. We were all staring at Murphy, waiting for the rest of his warning. He cleared his throat and smiled slightly. "You will know in due time," he whispered. "She will reveal herself on the next Eve of The Harvest." And that was the end of it.

With the distraction of the pregnancy over the next 8 months and then the process of settling in with our new child, that conversation had been mostly not discussed between us. During my many hours alone practicing from the Book of Magic and Spells, I had often thought of it and had felt the urgency to learn and perfect my skills. I had shrewdly passed on much of those lessons to them both through silly games and weekly "Family Training" days. Tomorrow is Thanksgiving.

Chapter Three

It was just after dusk and now officially "The Eve of The Harvest." I had felt a growing dread for most of the day and I nearly jumped out of my skin when there was a knock on the front door just as it became dark outside. "You must be Daddy," the slender little redhead giggled as I opened the door. "I'm Amanda," she added as she stepped into the house.

"You must be Casey!" She leaned forward to kiss my cheek. *"I am so...going to fuck your brains out!"* I heard it very clearly in my mind. She reached around and squeezed on my rump.

"Mommies main squeeze!" She laughed her taunt. Roni and Roz were now standing at the entrance to the foyer. They had heard her boastful claim as clearly as I had. We all knew in this moment that our trouble had arrived.

As I glanced over at my two brides, I was again smitten by how truly beautiful they look together. I noticed a look of curiosity on Amanda's face when she noticed that they were holding hands. *"He must be quite something if he has convinced them to do a threesome!"* I saw a smile grow on Veronica's face as we all heard what Amanda had thought. "He is much more than you can ever imagine!" I saw Amanda flinch as she realized that her mother had read her thoughts.

The three of us had practiced for this moment for the last six months. We had gotten the idea shortly after I painted the wall behind the baby's crib. I painted it a soft sky blue with little white flying sheep with wings. We used the image to transmit peace and contentment whenever he was upset or crying.

Amanda suddenly felt a little odd. She knew that she *should* be feeling apprehension because she could no longer read her mother's mind. It had always been so effortless in the past. But now she was feeling an intense feeling of wellbeing. There was absolute silence. And....SHEEP? Little white fluffy flying sheep with wings against a beautiful soft blue sky.

"Let me introduce myself." Amanda heard a soft angelic voice within her head. *"I am The Wizard...Casey Emeress."* She had clearly heard his voice and yet his lips had not moved.

"THE WIZARD...CASEY EMERESS," it finally reached her reasoning. "Oh My God, A Wizard?, You Are A Wizard?" Her voice cracked slightly as she said the words.

"Welcome home, Amanda!" This time she heard his voice as he said the words out loud. She saw him leaning forward to kiss her forehead. Her knees nearly buckled as she felt the warmth of his lips pressed against her. There was a jolt. Like a discharge of static electricity. Except it felt like a thousand volts had discharged into her brain.

Amanda felt like running. And yet, she wanted to wrap her arms around him and never let go. A supernova of heat swept through her body and it felt like time stood still. It only lasted a few moments but it felt like an eternity. It was the most extraordinary sensation of bliss that Amanda had ever experienced. Every particle of her being wanted to connect with him. *"I must have you!"* It was her first conscious thought as time seemed to resume. It was a deep consuming need.

She heard the two women laughing merrily. Their voices resonated deep within her brain. It was as if their voices were intertwined as they danced inside her mind. She felt like she should be angry with them. Yet, their voices were so joyful and angelic that she felt connected to them.

As Casey stepped back, Amanda suddenly became aware of the hot fluid running down her legs and pooling on the floor between her feet. She had just wet herself. Her bladder had emptied itself in one torrential gush. The acrid smell of her urine quickly filled the small entryway hall.

She had not noticed that he had taken her hand and was now leading her into the living room. She thought it a bit strange that she didn't feel even remotely embarrassed about wetting herself. She marveled at that consuming sense of serenity that seemed to radiate throughout her entire being. *"I don't know what got into me."* It was almost a fleeting thought that was unspoken.

Veronica and Rosalind had stopped laughing but their smiles told her that they knew exactly what had gotten into her. They knew exactly how consuming and addicting this connection felt. They knew exactly how desperately she needed this bliss...this man. They knew that she would never be able to go back...be satisfied...be without him.

"This is my son Daxx," I introduced my son to Amanda as Rosalind began to nurse him at the dinner table. She got a funny look on her face. "I thought...you married...Mom." I could hear the curiosity in her voice. "I married them both!" I chuckled my reply. They both smiled at her coyly. "YOU...will be my third!" I said it as a matter of fact.

Wizard Murphy had come to see us last week. He told us that the time of our trouble was very near. He told us it was imperative that I bond with and marry Amanda so that when the real trouble begins she would be somewhat manageable. He confided to us that future trouble would be with her children. Twins...a boy and a girl. They would both be gifted and nearly as powerful as their father....me.

He cautioned us that we must not ever let Amanda be bonded to my other two wives. She would then have less power over them which would keep them at advantage which will be important once the children are grown. It would also keep her from having any power over Daxx.

"That could be crucial later in life," he warned us.

Before he left, he made it very clear that time was of the essence. He informed us that I should be certain to bond with her within the first

24 hours and that the marriage should be within the first week while she is still under the spell we had cast and controllable by her own desires.

By the time we finished dinner, it was obvious that Amanda was suffering from the Jet lag and extremely sleepy from her long flight from Paris where she has been attending college. It is also where she has continued learning her Sorcery from a wannabe Wizard name Sam. Although he has been very savvy at teaching her spells and chants that he gleaned from books, he has no real powers of his own since he was not born gifted. Because of this, she will never be any more powerful than Veronica and Rosalind. And since they are equally bonded to my Power, they will always have the upper hand with her.

Veronica took her upstairs to help her get ready for bed. *"You won't mind...that I am going to... have him too?"* Amanda's voice sounded soft and sincere when she asked it. But Roni could clearly feel the secret boastful joy inside of her daughter. The thrill that she was going to mate with her Mother's husband. *"Are you sure you won't mind being third?"* Roni couldn't resist the opportunity for her own little barb. *"But I'm sure you will be....special to him...in your own way!"* She added the last knowing that Amanda would believe her youth and sexuality would give her an advantage over me in some manner.

Amanda smiled wickedly to herself as soon as her mother left. *"I'll show you!"* she thought to herself as she stepped over to the full length mirror across from the bed. *"I'm going to fuck him tonight...my very first night in this dump!"* She stepped closer to the mirror and slowly began to remove her clothes. Enjoying the reflection of her own beauty as each part of her body became exposed.

Amanda was fully aware that her young body is not as full and voluptuous as her Mothers or Rosalind's. Although she has the same wavy red hair, emerald green eyes and milky white skin as her mother, her frail petite body is completely different in every other way. She is almost five inches shorter and her figure is more like you would expect to find on a girl in her early teens. She is certain that her fresh nubile body will be irresistible to Casey. Her perfect little cone shape titties with the pink puffy nipples will be delightful to him.

"I may be a little tired...but I can still do this," she whispered to herself. Amanda put on a very transparent, white Baby Doll nightie, fixed her hair into cute little pigtails and crawled onto the bed. For several moments she recited her favorite seduction enchantment. Saying Casey's name over and over. Envisioning him fondling her, kissing her and mounting her. She was also slowly working her fingers up and down her smooth bare slit to get herself aroused and ready for him.

"I guess she took the bait!" Rosalind giggled when we began to feel Amanda's arousal. Roni was not able to feel a thing. There is an automatic block between parents and their children that prevents any feeling of sexual arousal or sexual interest. That has been so since the beginning of time for those gifted and even for those who have learned the craft.

Roz and I could clearly hear the soft chants, we could feel her arousal and we could feel her greedy lust. *"She's going to fuck your brains out!"* Roz giggled. *"I guess that Roni and I will just have to entertain each other tonight,"* she teased as she leaned over to kiss me on the cheek.

I kissed them both on the cheek before I left the kitchen. They decided to spend the night in the protected basement to prevent them from having to hear or feel our sexual bonding up in the second master bedroom. They did not want to feel connected to her in that way. *"We'll have breakfast ready for you in the morning!"* Veronica tried to sound cheerful. *"Try to get SOME sleep!"* She taunted me coyly.

I was pleased that the girls had chosen to not listen in on this first encounter with Amanda. I had already made up my mind what I would do with her this first time. I could feel her cockiness welling up inside of her as I tapped lightly on the bedroom door. So convinced that her weak little enchantment had succeeded for her. She seemed genuinely pleased when I left the door wide open as I slowly made my way to the bed.

was tenderly kissing her neck and fondling her perky little tits. "Do you want me to stop now?" I asked her very softly.

'Oooh No… Oh …GOD NO," she bellowed. Her legs wrapped around my waist snugly as if to emphasize her intention. "Fuck me...Fuck me...Fuck me," she grunted as she humped her hips up to meet my downward thrusts. I could now feel her arousal radiating through me. I was now connected with her as I had been the first time I had mated with Roni and then Roz. Now, I lifted the spell and allowed her to feel it too. I let her feel my lust. I let her feel all the physical sensations that were vibrating back and forth between us.

Amanda's eyes were wide open now as I gazed into her deepest thoughts and sensations. "Ooooh Casey...I never...dreamed...it could be like this!" Her voice was a deep throaty lust filled moan. I could feel her body beginning to shudder and the heat radiating from deep inside her womb was pulsating through both of us like a tidal wave. "I'm going to cum," she groaned.

As her body started to convulse beneath me, I was flooded with her emotions as well as her physical sensations. For the first time, her selfishness and pride fell away and for a moment, I felt the most overwhelming sensation of rapturous joy that I had ever encountered. "Oooh Casey, Oooh Yesss!" As my seed flooded into her womb her entire body seemed to melt into mine. There was brilliant white light that surrounded us for just a moment as I filled her belly with my semen.

"It is done...we are mated," I let her hear my voice inside her head. *"You will have Twins...a Girl and a Boy."* There were tears in her eyes as I rolled off of her. She reached over and gently held my hand as we laid there and rested side by side. "Will it always...be like that?" she asked softly. I tenderly brushed the hair from her face. *"That depends on the give and take!"* My angelic voice whispered into her brain. *"When you want to give yourself, it will be tender...but when you want to take, it will be rough!"* I leaned over and kissed her gently on the cheek "It's up to you!" I told her in a soft voice.

It was just after midnight when I slid off the bed. Amanda was in such a deep sleep that she was out cold. I stood there a moment and gazed at her frail nubile body. Despite her defiance, her proudness and rebellious streak, I find myself very fond of her already and quite sexually attracted. Something I will have to keep a handle on in the future.

I took a quick shower and headed down stairs. I found Veronica in the kitchen sipping a cup of Herbal tea. "I couldn't sleep!" She blushed a little as she said it. I took her by the hand and pulled her to her feet. "Let's go somewhere private," I whispered as I kissed her cheek. I led her out the back door and over to cottage number one. It was just beginning to snow.

In the protection of the stone cottage, no one else would be able to hear or feel our passion. *"This must be quite a conquest for you...Mother and Daughter in the same night?"* She thought it in a teasing way, but I could feel her uncertainty and self-doubt. "You will always be my first Love, Roni!" I said the words out loud. "That's why I am with you right now!" I bent forward and kissed her very passionately. I could feel her melting into my arms. I could feel her uncertainty fading away. I made love to her very tenderly that night. We slept together very peacefully.

Chapter Four

The wedding was set for the Saturday right after Thanksgiving. Murphy had insisted that we do it as quickly as possible. Before Amanda might get over being so enthralled with me. In his effort to insure that Veronica and Rosalind would not become bonded with Amanda, he also had insisted that Amanda and I come alone to the Monastery. Although they both understood this requirement, I could feel disappointment that they would have to be away from me.

On Thanksgiving Day, I made it a point to make some time for Rosalind and I to be alone. Although Veronica figured out what I was doing, Amanda never caught on. While Roni kept Amanda busy making preparations for our evening harvest meal, I snuck Roz out to Cottage number 4. I could feel that Roz was very pleased that I brought her there. There was certain giddiness as I closed the door behind us.

"I have loved you the longest!" I whispered it as I pulled her into my arms. "I longed to be with you for many years." It felt lovely as she began to kiss me passionately in return. *"I would do anything for you!"* Her thought let me know that she already knew what I was going to ask of her. *"I just wanted you to know how despicable I feel to ask this of you!"* She playfully squeezed my rump. "You're going to waste our time talking all day?" her voice was a coy taunt.

We spent the next two hours making love. It was not the usual lust filled frenetic forceful kind that we so often enjoy together. It was very slow, tender and endearing. By the time she arched her back and climaxed for the last time, we felt a renewed connection, a renewed bond that was ours alone. *"I'll be the best buddy she's ever had,"* She whispered into my brain as we were getting dressed to return. "Who knows...she might even be fun...to seduce," she added aloud.

The Thanksgiving dinner turned out lovely. This year I had three beautiful women waiting on me hand and foot. Each one giving me all of their attention and whispering little sweetnesses in my ear when the others were not paying attention. I got a kick out of the whole charade since I knew that they could ALL hear every thought being transmitted.

There was a blue wall with flying sheep in my mind as the game continued well into the evening. It was as if they were now in it together. All of them determined to say exactly the right thing to bring down the wall. *"It's my turn to fuck you!"* Amanda just blurted it out loud in her own brazenness. As the wall disappeared, it was revealed to all that I had fucked Veronica early in the morning and Rosalind in the afternoon.

"Looks like you won!" Rosalind announced softly. The smiles and playfulness had left her face and Veronica was no longer pleased either.

Amanda seemed surprised that they were now displeased. "Any cost...is usually very, very costly!" I whispered to her. "And sometimes the damage is hard to repair." As I stood up to accompany her upstairs I glared at her. "That is a lesson you should consider... the next time you wish to say something so stupid!"

Amanda practically flew up the stairs towards the room. I turned towards the girls and let them see and feel my displeasure with Amanda. For a moment there was a strange sensation that filled the living room. It was the sort of emotional turbulence that often happens with siblings. That quirky mixture of guilty pleasure that happens when one gets punished for a misdeed. They were both pleased that is wasn't them that had messed up but also felt guilty because they felt that pleasure. *"She earned this all by herself!"* They seemed relieved as soon as they saw the pained expression on my face.

Amanda was already naked on the bed when I entered her room. She was still trying to play a game with me. There was blue sky and flying sheep in her mind as I quietly closed the door behind me. She had seen the wall in Daxx's room earlier in the day and figured out how all three of us use that image to block thoughts. She seemed pleased with herself as I stood there next to the bed staring at her nakedness.

Her face quickly became shocked surprise as the sheep in her imagining fell from the wall and the blue sky evaporated. I noticed that she suddenly pulled the blanket up to cover her nakedness. She felt so exposed since I could hear her every thought and feel her every emotion.

I did not hide my displeasure from her. I let her feel all of it as well as my empathy for the hurt feelings that she had caused Veronica and Rosalind.

I was startled to find buried deep inside of her an overwhelming need to please me. A very deep desire to be loved by me. An unquenchable need to have me. I had followed her upstairs with every intention of punishing her for her rude self-centeredness. But now I realized it was an opportunity to teach. An opportunity to provide the loving encouragement of a man that she has never had. An opportunity to bond with her emotionally.

I felt her flinch slightly as I gently placed my hand on her right thigh. *"Right now is your chance to walk away."* My soft musical voice filtered into her consciousness. She let go of the blankets and moved her hand on top of mine. In that moment I knew she would not leave. *"If you truly want to be my wife, you need to be kind to my other two loves...you need to accept and respect them!"*

I paused a moment to allow that thought to sink in. *"They allowed you your privacy last night, but you violated theirs this evening!"* I reached forward and lifted her chin so she had to look me in the eyes. "That cannot ever happen again!" I said it softly. I could tell by the sheepish look on her face that she had felt my sincerity. She had also felt the new closeness that I now felt for her inside myself.

"You're not...going to...fuck my ass?" she asked me cautiously. That had been my intention as I entered the room. "No...we'll save that for some day when you want me to," I chuckled. "But I was a Bad Girl," she said it in a cute nasty sort of voice. I playfully rolled her over and slapped her hard on the ass. "Oooh YES!" her voice trembled with excitement. I slapped her a second time as I removed my clothes. I was delighted when she wet herself and the bed.

As I rolled her onto her back and crawled up between her legs, I heard a soft giggling in my mind from the girls downstairs. I also felt a great affection emanating from them. Like a joyous approval that I had found a way to teach rather than punish. As I glanced down at Amanda, I saw on her face that she heard it too and felt it too. *"Shall we let them in?"* she whispered in my head.

"Ooooh My God Yes," she gasped as I slowly slid my cock all the way up into her pussy. I could feel the girls shudder downstairs as they felt it too. Amanda seemed electrified by the sensation of their arousal as they felt me mounting her. "Soooo Good... Soooo good," she purred.

I slowly seesawed in and out of her dripping pussy and reveled in the waves of pleasure I was feeling as all three of them became more and more aroused.

I kissed her very passionately and sucked gently on her neck. The feelings of absolute bliss that flowed out from her was spectacular. I could feel her giving every part of herself to me as I began to tenderly suck on her breasts. This was a moment of bonding that would be so very important to us in the distant future. I could feel an overwhelming sense of joy as Veronica and Rosalind felt it too.

The conscious awareness of the three of them all reaching orgasm simultaneously was magnificently extraordinary. For a moment in time we were all connected, melded as one and joined together in a tidal wave of exquisite rapture. As my cock began to spasm and fill Amanda with my seed, there was a glow between us and time stood still for just a split second. "You will always be my Special Princess!" I whispered it softly as I fell forward and kissed her tenderly.

As we laid there resting for the minutes afterward, I could feel the radiating of her love as she replayed that term of endearment over and over in her mind. That deep need inside was being filled more sweetly than she had ever expected. I could feel the years of defiant loneliness begin to melt away. Her entire being seemed to surrender to that joy. *"Let that be a lesson to you, Bad Girl!"*Her giggle was a soft melodic joy that resonated deep in my heart.

I spent the entire night with Amanda that night. I could feel the approval from downstairs as Veronica and Rosalind were getting ready to go to bed. *"We Love you, Daddy."* They whispered into my thoughts. I saw a faint smile on Amanda's face as I pulled her up on top and began to kiss her. She reached between my legs and guided me into her sloppy wet vagina. *"Fuck me Daddy,"* she giggled playfully.

I knew that the girls had gone to the basement when I could no longer hear them of feel their presence within. I could tell that Amanda felt appreciative that she had me all to herself. *"Take me, Casey...make me all yours,"* she moaned softly. I could feel how deeply she wanted to be special to me.

I raised my head and began to nibble her perky conical breasts. *"You are the only one who has ever given me her virginity."* I swirled my tongue around one of her nipples. I felt her quiver as that sensation added to the intimacy of my remark. *"You will always be my Princess."*

Smack, smack, smack, smack...her ass slapped against my thighs as she pounded down onto my prick harder and harder. I could feel that her pussy was getting wetter and wetter and the heat of her passion was radiating through the both of us like a wildfire. As I gently bit into her left nipple our bodies both vibrated as one and my cock exploded into her as she jerked and spasmed with each of my four ejaculations. It was as if we climaxing as one entity. It was a truly amazing sensation.

There was an entirely new air in the house that next morning. Veronica and Rosalind were already in the kitchen cooking breakfast when Amanda and I came down from our shower together. "We were starting to think that the Honeymoon had started before the wedding!"

Roz chuckled her teasing remark.

I was very happy when Veronica came over and hugged Amanda warmly. "Welcome home, honey...welcome to your new family!" Inside I could feel the deep sincerity of her words. I could feel the very deep love of a mother for her daughter. I could feel how relaxed everyone had become and that wonderful feeling of wellbeing that had existed before our new addition. "Would you like some pancakes...Princess?" Roni asked playfully. We all got a chuckle out of that.

I noticed that they both got a sly little grin when they saw the couple of hickeys that I had put on the left side of Amanda's neck. Then there were giggles as they saw the couple she had given me in return. "Looks like you two were in a grape fight last night!" Veronica giggled. I saw Amanda blush a little as she laughed at her Mother's quip. It felt wonderful to feel the joy and amusement. It was good to see the tenseness melting away.

Later in the day that day, while Daxx was taking his afternoon nap, Amanda and I suddenly became aware of their arousal. Although Amanda could not feel her Mother's arousal, she could feel the passion, the lust and the physical pleasures inside of Rosalind. They were obviously having sex with each other in the Master Bedroom upstairs.

"Oh God...what should we do?" I could feel her curiosity. I could also feel that she was becoming very aroused by the sensations that she was experiencing. *"I think we should do this..."* I picked her up and kissed her passionately as I carried her to the couch. *"We should enjoy all these wonders that present themselves!"* I could feel her trembling as I removed her blouse and started fondling her perky little tits.

It felt wonderful to feel her excitement and arousal as she experienced all of the sensations for the very first time. She seemed pleased to feel the sensation of Roz's breasts being sucked. She had several climaxes as I ate her pussy at the same time that she could feel Rosalind's being fingered and licked. I felt her entire body vibrate when my dick slid up into her sex. For the very first time she was able to feel what it felt like inside of Rosalind. She could hear Roz's soft moan of delight.

When Amanda climaxed that afternoon it was so intense that she wet herself again. Upstairs, Rosalind wet herself too. We could both hear them giggling up in the bathroom. It felt wonderful to feel all that happiness and comfort.

Chapter Five

Amanda was mostly quiet during the first half of the three hour drive down to the Monastery. I made it a point to keep some soft music on the radio and hummed along with the melodies. This was to keep her out of my head and me out of her.

"I appreciate the privacy." She finally broke the silence. "But it's no longer necessary now!" As I smiled and stopped humming, I glanced over at her. I was again smitten by how truly lovely her frail nubile body is. Her milky white skin so pure and silky smooth. She was now smiling broadly as she gazed at the bulge rising up in my jeans.

"Ooooh...Maybe that's why you have been keeping yourself so busy!" Her voice sounded joyfully pleased. "Maybe I should start humming again!" I teased her. She laughed merrily as she poked me on the right shoulder. "Don't you dare...I love it that I have that effect on you!" She let her hand fall to my lap and gently squeezed on my bulge. "I look forward to riding this later!" She purred as she moved her hand away.

I could feel the happiness deep in her heart that she was going to have me all to herself for the next week following the wedding. We had told her that Veronica and Rosalind would not join us for the wedding so that we could enjoy a private honeymoon together. Like the privacy that they had shared on their wedding night with me.

All three of us had recited that in our mind over and over for the three days before we told her. It was so ingrained into thinking by then that she had no problem believing its validity. In truth, there really was happiness in my heart that we would have this time alone together. Despite the possible dangers ahead, I have found myself becoming closer and closer with her with each day that we spend together. The bond that I feel with her is entirely different than what I have with Veronica and

Rosalind. There is a sweet innocence with her that is breathtaking.

"I really am In Love with you, Casey!" She said it softly as she turned towards me. I could see the glow of love on her face as she reached forward to touch my right forearm. "*I could never do anything to cause you harm!*" her inner voice drifted into my awareness. Although I could tell that she could feel the surprise inside me, I did not try to block it from her.

Amanda then told me that she knew that there was something bothering everyone. She said that she could feel a deep unnamable fear inside all of us. She told me that she knew that it was part of the reason that they did not come with us for the wedding. "I could tell that in their hearts that they were happy for us to have this time alone," she whispered "But I could also feel a deep sense of relief."

~~oOo~~

I let there be a silence for several moments to allow her to see that I would not deny that or try to block her from my thoughts. Then I made a decision that would allow me to be truthful with her and continue to be open with her. "I am extremely happy that we will have this time alone!" I could sense that she could feel the truth of that in my heart.

"The rest of it I will share with you tomorrow." I reached over and laid my hand on her thigh. The added contact would enhance her ability to feel the intended truth of that statement. "Today I just want to experience the joy of our wedding bond!" That was an absolute truth.

As Amanda laid her hand on top of mine, I could feel her acceptance. I could feel the deep innocence of her devoted love for me. I could feel her happiness. "*I have never trusted anyone the way that I trust you!*" Her lovely melodic voice melted into my thoughts. "*I hope that someday you will trust me that way too!*" She leaned forward and kissed me gently on the cheek.

Murphy was waiting for us out front of the Monastery when we arrived. He had that quirky wry grin on his face as we walked towards him hand in hand. At 6 foot 2 I am nearly a foot taller than Amanda and with her petite frailness, she almost looks like she could be my daughter. "Is she old enough for you?" Murphy taunted. "I'm twenty three!" Amanda replied defensively.

I could feel her curiosity that she could not read into Murphy's thinking. I have never been able to read his mind unless he decides to converse that way. Whenever I have attempted to peer inside, all I have ever experienced is a deep feeling of serenity and contentment. I have often wondered how it would be to feel that quiet inside. It has always amazed me how peaceful I feel inside whenever I am with him. I could tell by the way that Amanda was relaxing that she felt that too.

"You are with child!" He announced it softly and as a matter of fact. He reached over and gently touched Amanda's belly. I could feel the serenity radiating into her. "It will be twins...you have chosen their names already." I could feel that she was so calm inside that she had no doubt that he knew that... even though she had not discussed it with anyone. She seemed very pleased that he could feel that.

"Casey and I need to discuss some things in private," he announced softly. "The girls will show you around and get everything ready for dinner." He had gently held her arm so she could feel that there was no attempt to conceal anything from her. As if on cue, his four wives came out to greet us. I was surprised to see that Josie, his youngest wife, was pregnant. VERY pregnant. Within days of delivery pregnant.

I could hear Amanda giggling as they led her away. She seemed very attentive to whatever it was that Josie was saying to her. I could feel her excitement and a feeling of contentment. "My son is going to be...our insurance." Murphy whispered. He led me out to the stone cottage at the back of the property where Amanda and I will stay for the next week. "We can talk freely in here!" he reminded me as we entered the cottage.

"My son's name will be Carson." He said it so softly that I barely heard it. "Carson Murphy...that has a nice ring to it!" I told him cordially. I could see a very serious look on his face as he looked directly into my eyes. "Carson Emeress....my son is also your brother." As the depth of that statement flooded into me, Murphy laid his hand on my left arm. "You are my son, Casey... I am the Wizard Murphy Emeress."

I was stunned. Time literally stood still. As I glanced at the grandfather clock on the wall, the pendulum stopped in its upswing. I glanced out the window and there were two crows that were completely motionless, as if frozen in midair. It startled me when I felt Murphy remove his hand from my arm. Although everything else around us was frozen in time, we were still able to move, able to talk and able to feel everything around us.

Murphy spent the next two hours explaining things to me. He told me that when the Counsel of Wizards had discovered that he could stop time many years ago, they had cast him out. He told me that when they discovered that he and Sara, his first wife...my Mother, were expecting a child, they had ordered her to be executed.

He explained to me that when she heard of this, that she ran away in the middle of the night without telling him. Sara had managed to make it to a small town in Main and had given birth. She had listed the father as unknown and had me taken to an orphanage. When she returned home, the counsel executed her because she would not disclose my location.

There were tears in his eyes as he told me my entire life story. For the very first time, I did not feel that familiar zen like serenity. I could feel his pain. I could feel that deep love of a father for his son, I could feel the emptiness that had been caused by the loss of my mother. I could feel the relief that he was finally able open these things to me.

At the end of our very lengthy conversation, Murphy told me that I had made a very good choice to marry Amanda. He told me that the chance meeting with Veronica had been planned but that he had never imagined the depth of that relationship. He told me that the addition of

Rosalind had been a very fortuitous fluke that would strengthen everyone in our coven.

"But what has happened with you and Amanda was beyond even my ability to foresee," he confided. He explained that because of her history of rebellion and her propensity to be a loner that he had believed that it would be impossible to trust her when the Vexing begins. *"I never considered the power of love!"* It suddenly occurred to me that his voice sounded so much like my own inside my head. *"The change in her demeanor and her level of inner calmness is most remarkable!."* He reached over to touch my arm again. "It is her love for you that has allowed her to trust for the first time in her life!" I could hear the admiration in his voice as he said it.

~~oOo~~

"Can we make time resume now..I'm getting hungry?" I said it teasingly. He smiled at me with that wry smile of his. "That would be up to you, my son, you are the one who has stopped it," he chuckled softly. I glanced at the clock and the pendulum began to sway back and forth. We had talked for over three hours and yet it was only 5 minutes later when we walked into the main house.

"That was a quick talk!" Amanda exclaimed as she craned her neck up to kiss me on the cheek. As her lips touched my cheek, she felt the change immediately. No voices, no thoughts, no white flying sheep...just...absolute serenity. *"What has he done to you?"* I could feel her disappointment and a little bit of fear. As she whispered it into my thoughts.

"I will tell you everything My Love...as soon as we are bonded!" I let her hear my tranquil voice inside. "All is going to be well...just as it is intended!" I said it loud enough for everyone to hear. It was important that Murphy's wives understood that too. I could feel their uneasiness just as clearly as Amanda's.

Although they trust and rely on Murphy without question, they are still not so comfortable with me yet. "Everyone will be fine…we will all grow together nicely!" I opened myself to them so they could all feel the sincerity inside of my inner peace. I could feel them all begin to relax a little. "Now can we please eat dinner...I am starving!" I saw that wry grin on Murphy's face again.

It was about 9 p.m. when we all took our places in the Gazebo for the Wedding Ceremony. Amanda was stunning in an all-white lacy gown that Josie had lent her. There was a ring of flowers in her hair and she smelled like honeysuckle. The only makeup she had on was a cherry red lip gloss. I was thrilled with the freshness of my lovely young bride.

The girls again made those little starlight images in the sky. Wedding bells and interlocked hearts. There was again the soft angelic music. This time, as Amanda and I held hands, he had us face each other and we connected with both hands. *"Once this is done...you can never be parted...ever!"* I was surprised by his different wording. I could tell by the way that Amanda was squeezing my hands so tight, that she did not intend to ever be apart. "WE are ready, Father!"

I heard a gasp from all four of his wives as my words were heard. I felt a relaxing sensation within Amanda as if everything had just become clear for her and she welcomed that. With a nod of his head, the girls again started the wedding ritual chant. The same incoherent sentence over and over. Murphy placed one hand on my head and the other on the Master Book of Spells and Chants.

As he recited the wedding ritual, Amanda and I both began to radiate heat and glow from inside just like it had happened with Roni and Roz. But this time it became different. As the bright light became blindingly bright, all of the molecules seemed to separate and suddenly our two bodies became a ball of dazzling dots that were swimming around and intermixing together. Dancing and frolicking and uniting.

This was a special bond that Murphy had agreed to. He was hesitant at first, but I convinced him that this would create the trust and unbreakable bond in us that would carry us through any danger we would have to face in the future. In that moment, time again stood still and Amanda was filled with my entire lifetime of memories, feelings and emotions. I also experienced the same from her. In an instant, we became more one than is humanly possible.

When the molecules lifted from us and exploded into the sky, I could feel the tears in her eyes and she could feel mine. *"You do trust me!"* Her sweet voice flooded into my mind. As we kissed very passionately, I could feel the most overwhelming sense of love. It was a bonded devotion that felt magnificent and impenetrable. *"I am yours forever."* I could feel her joy.

When Veronica and Rosalind and I had mated for the first time after the wedding, it had been the most intensely exquisite experience that any of us had ever experienced. Nothing could have prepared me or Amanda for what would be our mating bond. The total and absolute connection to each other that had been created by the molecules of our shared consciousness, had truly melded us together more completely than I could ever have imagined.

As I slowly undressed my frail young bride, I could feel the total surrender of very part of her being. I could feel the excited joy that she desired to be mine in every way. Each time our bodies touched in anyway, little sparks lifted from us and floated away. We felt little tingles each time it happened and it raised little goose bumps on our skin. When our lips finally met, there was such a warm tingly sensation that it made us kiss hungrily for several minutes.

As a wedding present, Murphy had recreated Amanda's hymen. He had felt my guilt that I had caused her to burst her virginity with her own fingers. He had done this without telling me so it would not ruin the surprise for either of us. The heat and magnetism that we felt as I crawled on top of her nakedness was addictive.

There was a magnificent explosion of pain mixed with rapturous pleasure as my cock burst through her new virginity. I held myself buried inside of her for several long moments as that exquisite sensation of pain mixed with pleasure washed back and forth between us like storm surf in a hurricane.

There were tears of joy on both our faces as our bodies jerked and quivered as one. As I began to slowly make love to her, the overpowering feelings of love that radiated back and forth between us was so overwhelming that we both wept openly. It was like every cell and every neuron within us were joined together. Each of us is experiencing each instant as an orgasmic wave that invaded every part of us.

She could feel each pulsation of my cock throbbing deep within her. I could feel every spasm as her vaginal muscles contracted and retracted with each beat of her heart. We mated very slowly like this for nearly 45 minutes. As we reached our orgasm together, the supernova of tiny molecules were again swarming around us.

As Amanda began to convulse and my semen began erupt into her womb, the ball of fiery little dots exploded in one divine fission wave of unbridled passion. It swept through the both of us like an atomic blast that left us panting in each other's arms as it dissipated into a million little tingly embers of electric dust that fell to us and sprinkled its last heated discharge. *"I will never forget this,"* Amanda whispered softly into my awareness.

Amanda was amazed when she glanced at the clock and it had not moved in the entire forty five minutes of our mating. "Did you...do that?" she asked incredulously. I blinked once and smiled at her. "Did I do what?" I replied coyly. When she again glanced at the clock it was now forty five minutes later. I allowed her to feel the playfulness inside so she would know that she had been right. I also allowed her to know that she was the only one besides Murphy and Me that knew I could stop time. Our trust building was now complete.

Chapter Six

Murphy was in the kitchen alone when we came to the house the next morning. "The girls have gone with Josie, it is her time," he informed us when we noticed he was alone. "You will have a brother by noon." Although we could feel just the overpowering sensation of serenity that is so familiar with him, we could also see the love in his eyes and the pride of fatherhood.

"He will be very special...just like you, Casey!" I could also feel his love for me. So did Amanda. As Murphy brought our breakfast to us from the stove, I noticed a new Master Book of Spells and Chants on the table in front of us. There was also a very shiny black lacquered stick that was lying next to it. A twelve inch Wand. *"The book is for your mate,"* he chuckled when he saw my surprise. *"The other is for you...take good care of it!"* For a moment I could feel a little merriment inside of him.

As I began to reach for the wand, it suddenly jumped from the table and into my grasp. There was a huge crackling noise, like the sound of thunder and a flash of light. It felt like my hand had just been struck by lightning. The excruciating pain was for just an instant and then replaced with a soothing wave like a cool Autumn breeze. *"Now you are bonded to it for life,"* we both heard the amusement in his voice. "Now...we can eat!" he laughed.

Murphy told us that he would meet us in the cottage out back when we finished breakfast. He told us to take our time. "I'm sure you would like to make use of the larger shower in the Master Bedroom!" We could feel a bit of naughty playfulness in his remark. The sex in the shower that morning was as torrid as any other we had shared in the past. But it was not nearly as prolific as that first bonding last night. "Back to just incredible," Amanda teased me as we dried off. We both giggled and kissed again tenderly. "I can settle for incredible," I whispered in her ear softly.

~~oOo~~

Murphy was waiting for us inside the cottage when we finally went looking for him. I could feel Amanda's relief that she had made the bed and tidied up before we had gone to the house for breakfast. A detail I would not have thought of. "This is your first lesson," Murphy grumbled as I came in the door. "Never leave your wand unattended!" he exclaimed. I glanced at the table where I had left it before I had gone to join Amanda in the shower. It was not there.

Murphy crossed his arms and smiled slyly. "Now you are going to have to find it!" He seemed pleased with himself. I thought for a moment and remember that the wand was bonded to me. "Come to me wand!" I commanded. Nothing happened. "It doesn't work that way...but you know that," his voice was playful now. "Think, Son...you know how to do this!" The certainty in his voice told me that I should know this already. I had a momentary remembrance of moving that tree out back of Veronica's lodge. I envisioned the shiny black wand resting in my hand.

As I felt the weight of the stick in my hand, I glanced over at Murphy expecting his praise and encouragement. "Now...practice that the rest of today," he grumbled again. "See if you can teach your Princess how to do it too!" His voice playful again. I could feel a bit of temper rising inside of Amanda. She was not amused that he had used my pet name for her. "There are no secrets in a coven, young lady!" He turned and faced us again. "That is the other lesson...you must never forget it!"

Amanda and I spent the rest of the afternoon practicing the craft of moving objects. I found that with some practice, I was able to make certain things disappear and reappear. Although Amanda became fairly proficient at moving things, she was not able to get the hang of making things disappear. There had been several blunders and mistakes during the first part of the practicing. Several dishes got broken, several heavy pans hit the floor, and an errant zap from my wand blew a small hole in the stone wall of the cottage. There was much laughter and giggling throughout the day. Though we were both working hard at getting better at our tasks, we managed to have a very enjoyable time of it and our bond felt even sweeter.

It was just becoming dusk as we made our way back from the woods where we had gone to practice on larger items and experience different obstacles. As we neared the cottage I saw a small tree branch in our path and had a sudden fleeting thought. I had Amanda stop and I told her to hold out her hands. I envisioned the branch raising and resting in her open palms.

As the branch gently lowered into her hands, there was just enough weight in the branch that it took her undivided attention to hold it up. I saw the bewildered look on her face as she suddenly heard my next intention. "Oooh...you…wouldn't!" the words were just out as her pants fell to her knees. She was standing there fully exposed from her waist to her knees since she had not worn panties.

~~oOo~~

I found that it was difficult to run while I was belly laughing. Amanda quickly had dropped the branch, pulled up her pants and was now pelting me with stones that she willed to fly off the ground in my direction. We both stopped in our tracks when one of them inadvertently struck me just above my left eye. It caused a three inch gash just above my eyebrow that bled profusely. Murphy was able to repair the wound once we got to the house. But there would be a permanent scar.

Amanda was amazed that during the entire ordeal she had never felt anything but calmness and serenity inside of me. During the same period of time she was feeling a deep remorse and guiltiness that she had caused me such pain and created a scar for life.

I could hear her wondering about my ability to remain so peaceful during such a painful and traumatic event. "Calm thoughts!" I whispered as we entered the cottage. I could feel her skepticism as she smiled wryly. I reached over and laid my hand on her arm so she would be able to understand. *"It was a gift left for me by my mother!"* I felt her relaxing as my thoughts made their way into hers.

My mother's gift had been her ability to keep an immense serenity within her under any circumstance. It was that ability that had enabled her to keep my location safe even when she had been tortured. Shortly after her death, Murphy had found a potion that she had left for him. She had created it with her own DNA so that Murphy would be able to make use of it and, someday, pass it on to me.

I could feel the hopeful curiosity inside of Amanda even though she was trying to stifle it. "It will last my entire life," I let it seem like an afterthought to allow her to think she had blocked her curiosity. "And, unfortunately, it cannot be taught!" By the time I withdrew my hand from her, she had calmed considerably. She now also understood that I could, however, transmit the calmness to others by touch.

I could still feel a deep regret inside of her as we were getting ready for bed that evening. I kissed her tenderly on the cheek. *"It's OK my love...I look at it as if you have marked your territory!"* I whispered it into her mind. *"It is my badge of honor!"* I added. I felt a glimmer of a smile as she considered my intention.

I could hear her request before she even said it. "Could you...mark me somehow...too?" I could feel her genuine desire to have my mark on her…that she could too have her badge of honor. I reached over and pressed on her upper thigh just inches from her pubic area with my right index finger. I felt her flinch as a momentary sharp pain shot into her flesh. When I lifted my finger she had an identical jagged scar just inches from her sex.

Amanda shrieked with delight when saw what I had done. She pushed me back onto the bed and crawled on top of me. She was giggling as she smothered me with kisses. I could feel how truly in love she is with me and the joy that we were marked together. "I am all yours forever!"

As if to prove her statement, she kissed her way down my body.

"Oooh yes!" My legs vibrated as she began to suck my cock. The sensation of my prick swelling to full rigidity in her hot wet mouth was marvelous. Gluck, gluck, gluck, gluck…she made little gagging noises as she forced my 9 inch dick further and further into her throat. When she would lift her head to gasp for air, long strands of gooey saliva oozed down from her chin onto my belly and thighs.

I was absolutely electrified by the deliciously nasty sensation of her deep throating my oozing dick. I desperately wanted her to climb up and fuck me. But I was so lost in the pleasure that she was giving me, the best I could do is pant and groan her name over and over. As I felt my nutsack tingling near orgasm, Amanda pulled my cock out of her mouth and began to jerk me off between her perky cone shaped tits.

"Oooh YES...YESSSSS...GOD YESSSSS!" I screamed as my cock erupted three times. My semen sprayed up into her face and all over her breasts. She was laughing joyously as she felt my slippery hot cream shooting out all over her. "This is your territory too," she said it in a naughty sort of tone as she drug my dick back and forth across her cum drenched tits. "I will always be your territory!" She scooted up and kissed me very passionately.

I could hear a soft giggling from the shower as I slowly awoke in the morning. As I slowly became aware of my surroundings, I suddenly realized that I could not move. Somehow, my hands and feet had been tethered to the four bedposts. *"I have a surprise for you!"* I hear her soft playful voice in my head.

She was now standing in the doorway of the bathroom totally naked. In her left hand, she had a plastic bottle of oil. In her other hand, she was holding my wand. Although she was covering her intentions by humming to herself, I could feel that her intent was playful and that she was not going to harm me in anyway. I decided to let her have her way even though I could easily make the ropes holding me dissolve.

"We have a score to settle," she giggled as she crawled onto the bed and sat on my thighs. As she began to pour the oil all over my genitals, I understood what she had in mind. "Oh honey, that's not a good idea," I gasped as she reached down and began to stroke my rigid piss hard on.

"I have to pee, sweetie....I have to pee!" Amanda scooted up so that my cock was right up against her pussy. As she masturbated my slick cock, her fingers also brushed up and down her slippery sex hole. She was stroking herself as she jerked me off. *"You made my pants fall down yesterday...that was very naughty!"* Her soft voice sounded joyously seductive in my thoughts.

"Oh my God this feels good," she moaned as her fingers aroused her sex while she beat me off. *"You made my pussy all wet...then left me standing there with a tree branch stuck in my hands!"* Her body shivered as she felt herself getting close to orgasm. I could feel her climax as it built to an incredible crescendo of explosive release.

Just as her body began to jerk and quiver, my cock exploded with her. My cum shot up and sprayed all over her belly and down onto my thighs. As she bucked back and forth, she was still continuing to jerk my cock.

"AMANDA...I HAVE TO...I HAVE TOO..." it felt like my entire body was electrified as the over sensitiveness caused my bladder to empty itself.

"OH MY GOD...OH MY GOD...OOOOH MY GOD!" I screamed as my body convulsed uncontrollably. Four huge blasts of urine gushed out of my prick.

The first two blasts sprayed all over my body and even up into my face. Then she pulled my cock back so the last two gushes sprayed all over her. *"Remember making me wet myself that first night?"* There was a sweet amusement deep within her. "Now you wet the both of us!" she laughed gleefully as she finally let go of my prick.

Amanda and I spent the rest of the week out in the woods each day practicing. I mostly taught her the spells that I was already familiar with. And I practiced using my new wand. There was also a certain amount of playfulness each day. And there was a break each afternoon for what we called "Back to Nature Time". That meant that we got naked and had torrid sex right there in the middle of nature.

It was just after our Back to Nature break on Friday afternoon when we heard the twig breaks of approaching footsteps. We were both still half naked when Murphy appeared from behind the tree. "Sorry to intrude on your grab ass session," he grumbled. "But I wanted to talk to you alone before your leave tomorrow!"

In his left hand there was a wand similar to the one he had given me. Except the special embellishment on the barrel was different. On my wand, there are four cobras etched along the length. On the other wand there were dozens of tiny black widow spiders. He handed it to Amanda. "This is yours!" He said it as if it has always been so.

In his right hand he was holding two small books. They were books of instruction on how to use the wands properly. When I glanced at him with curiosity, he took my wand and chanted a short spell. The cobra's suddenly disappeared from my wand and came to life as four live cobra's coiled on the ground about fifteen feet in front of us. Then he chanted a different sort of incantation and they reappeared on my wand.

I could feel the thrill inside of Amanda as he demonstrated with her wand. There suddenly appeared a large swarm of hundreds of black widow spiders. When he had finished, she threw herself into his arms and kissed him on the cheek. "That will be enough of that!" he growled as he pulled away from her. "And put some clothes on!"

Amanda had forgotten that she was still completely topless. Her perky breasts had been mashed against Murphy's chest. I could feel his embarrassed befuddlement that he was now fully erect. I could also feel his relief when she turned away without noticing as she went to put her top back on. I averted my gaze in an attempt to lessen his embarrassment.

Murphy had managed to compose himself as we sat on the log together and watched Amanda finish dressing herself. "The black widows on her wand represent the nature of her gift," he whispered. "She is a true temptress of the same sort!" His voice betrayed his displeasure that he had gotten aroused.

"And here I thought that I had enchanted her!" I said it playfully. He smiled at me knowingly. "Because of the nature of her gift, she is immune to any sort of spell or enchantment of seduction!" He informed me. As he saw the look of concern growing on my face, he reached over and patted me on the shoulder. "Fortunately for you, all of those feelings inside of her are genuine!" He added.

Murphy and I had both composed ourselves by the time that Amanda joined us sitting on the log. All was again peaceful and serene. "I have something to tell you that is important to our future...all of us." His said it in a soft but serious tone. "It is both good news and bad," he added. Over the next several minutes, he about the future danger that we will all be faced with. He told us the Veronica, a "seer of the future," had contacted him just days after we had first met. She had called to warn him of the vision she had just experienced.

Her vision had revealed to her that we would be married and that Rosalind would join us in wedlock bearing a son. She had foreseen that Amanda would become my third wife and bear twins. But the rest of the vision had been vague. All that she was able to see at that time was that there would be a grave danger ahead and that the twin girl would somehow be involved.

Murphy then informed us that Veronica had just recently experienced a new vision. He told us that Kira, our daughter, would not "be" the danger but would create the problem due to an unforeseen action that she would be forced to take. He disclosed that her action would create a problem with the "Counsel of Thirteen." that would be similar to what had happened with my mother so many years ago.

We were all very quiet during the walk back to the Monastery. Underneath my veil of peace and serenity, I was quite relieved that I would no longer need to hide anything from my Amanda anymore. I was happy that I could now be as open with her as with Veronica and Roz. Inside of Amanda, I could feel that she felt worried about the future. But she felt comforted in her understanding of the future. She felt even more connected to me.

We all spent the evening in the Monastery together. We had a wedding party of sorts. Now that everyone was certain that Amanda was in the same situation as the rest of us, there was a much more open exchange of camaraderie and acceptance. I had taken some time earlier in the evening explaining everything to her. I was very grateful that she understood the gravity of the things I had hidden from her. I was also very pleased that she could feel the depth and sorrow about having been closed off to her. I was greatly relieved that her love had not swayed in the least. We had come through this together and it had bonded us even deeper.

Amanda was especially affectionate with me the rest of the evening. Even Murphy and his four wives had noticed her constant touching and petting that night. They noticed the sparkle in her eyes and the goofy look on her face. The expression one gets when totally enraptured.

Now that she had been exposed to every particle of my being, every thought and desire, she was flooded with the joy of that trusted connection with me. Amanda had always believed that I would bond with her this completely. But she had always assumed that it would be due to her youth and beauty. She could not have ever guessed that I would fall in love with everything about her.

"I never knew it could be like this," she told me when we finally went back to the cottage to get ready for bed. "I never knew anything could feel this wonderful!" Her hand was trembling as she petted my arm softly. I could feel the passion of her love washing through her in waves. *"I am so happy with you, My Love,"* she whispered into my mind.

Smack, Smack, Smack, Smack...the sound of my body slamming against hers reverberated off the walls as I impaled her with my throbbing prick over and over. Her deep throaty grunts and gasps aroused me even deeper as I pounded into her harder and harder. "Take Me...Take Me...Take Me!" She bellowed as I felt her climax building within her.

Her body convulsed as her orgasm exploded throughout her entire being. The sensations of her bliss radiated through the both of us and sent me over the edge of rapture with her. As my cock erupted into her three heavy ropes of semen, we both convulsed together as one being.

"I love you, Princess," I whispered as I relaxed and let her legs fall back onto the bed. We slept very contented that night. Spooning and intertwined as one.

Amanda was more excited than I had ever seen her as we made the three hour drive home. Unlike the solemn trip one short week ago she chattered and giggled and petted me. I could feel her hopefulness and her deep conviction that together we can face the new chapter of our lives that lies ahead. Me, my coven and our children. More will surely be revealed...

To be continued...

Here is a sample from another story you may enjoy:

JACK RYDER

The Inn Keeper's Wizard

WHEN LOVE AND MAGIC COLLIDE...

Erotic Fantasy

I was hired by a very large insurance firm to be their Head Claims Adjustor. As the head representative, I rarely investigated small claims. I was mostly involved with large, catastrophic losses. The type of losses that are created by Tornados, Hurricanes, Earthquakes and any other losses associated with large-scale disasters.

Due to the nature of these catastrophic events, I would be required to stay in those locations for long periods of time. Sometimes it would be several weeks, and sometimes it would be for many months. I found the Bed and Breakfast arrangement to be an ideal accommodation for my long and arduous assignments.

I was dispatched this time to a ski resort town in one of the higher elevations in Utah. It was the beginning of winter and an avalanche had destroyed many homes in this community and also several local businesses. I arrived the day after the disaster and just managed to beat the next winter storm that was approaching.

I froze in place with my mouth hanging open when I first saw Veronica of "Veronica's Bed and Breakfast." She could absolutely be the twin sister of that lady that plays "Lady Heather" in the hit TV show *CSI*.

"My name is Veronica...Not Heather!" She said it playfully. She obviously saw the look on my face and has obviously been told many times that she looks like that certain actress.

"My Name...is...Casey." It came out as a stammer. "I'm here...to...adjust you." Now I was even more embarrassed that my sentence came out all wrong. Veronica laughed softly and stuck out her hand to shake mine.

"I could use some adjusting, Casey," she chuckled. Her warm hand felt soft as velvet as she placed it in mine. I felt a soft electrical shock just as we touched.

When I was dropped off by the taxi in front of her establishment, I had assumed that she would put me into one of the 4 cottages behind the main house.

"I have put you upstairs in the second master bedroom," she informed me as she withdrew her hand from mine. She started to turn towards the front desk, but then turned back. "By the way...you can call me Roni." She also mentioned that there were no other guests due to the avalanche.

I had been very proud of myself that I had not glanced at her large lovely breasts even once during our conversation. But as she turned towards the desk, I got an eyeful of them pressed against the tight cashmere sweater she was wearing. I would guess that they are about 36D and with the way her nipples poked against the fabric, I would also guess that she was not wearing a bra.

"Wow, those are gorgeous," I thought to myself.

As she walked towards the counter to fetch my room key, I got a terrific view of her perfect, full round ass. In her tight jeans it was marvelous.

"I think you will find the view very pleasing here," she said as she bent over the counter to pick something up. I could feel my dick beginning to wiggle as I gawked at her lovely ass.

"Yes...I think I will!" I replied slyly.

My mind was in hyperdrive envisioning all the things I would dearly love to do to that sexy rear end. I noticed that she had lifted her head and was glancing back at me. I'm pretty sure that she could see the bulge that was rising in my 501 jeans.

"I'll have to make sure to show you ALL the sights," she said in a soft, playful tone.

I was surprised when she came back and handed me a stack of towels and washcloths instead of a room key. "You won't need a key," she whispered. "I only let my personal guests stay upstairs," she informed me.

I took the towels and held them by my waist to block the bulge in my pants. "I am very flattered that you consider me a personal guest!" I WAS very flattered!

I could not take my eyes off her full, voluptuous body as she led me up the stairs. She has that Marilyn Monroe sort of shape that just exudes sexuality. The faint aroma of her perfume was sweet and smelled like lilacs. Her hips swayed back and forth as we made the climb up the stairs. I now had a full chubby throbbing in my jeans.

There were two very large master bedrooms upstairs. Her room was directly across from the room that I would be using. At the end of the hallway, there was a very large library/conference room.

"I have set that up for you to use for doing your business," she advised. Then she showed me to the huge bathroom that was just to the left of the library. "We will share this, but that should not be a problem." She said it casually.

I was startled when she turned around and kissed me on the cheek. "I'm happy to have you here, Casey," she whispered in my ear. "I think we'll get on very nicely!"

My brain was already changing her words to "get it on."

She giggled as she stepped back. "Yes...very nicely," she repeated. As she walked away, I wondered if she had read my mind just then.

At 38 years old, Veronica is exactly ten years older than me. But I find myself attracted to her more than any of the younger women that I have ever dated or even the ones I bedded for a one night stand. Her firm, 36-26-37 body is tantalizingly sensual. Her full pouty lips seem so plump and ready to kiss. Her emerald green eyes sparkle and seem to peer into my soul. Her very dark red hair reaches to the middle of her back. It is so dark that indoors it almost appears to be a dark brown. Like any true redhead, her skin is a milky white and seems like it would be as silky as a fine cream. I would guess with her soft white complexion that her nipples would be a light pink. I could feel a few drops of precum dripping into my jeans.

"Feel free to use the shower or hot tub anytime you like!" she called back to me as she descended the stairs.

I practically ran into my room and sat down at the foot of the huge King Size bed with the towels pressed against my lap. *"Get a grip, Casey,"* I thought to myself. *"You've known her for all of ten minutes and you are already pining after her like a smitten schoolboy,"* I chastised myself.

But my throbbing dick wasn't so sure it was a simple case of schoolboy yearning.

I found myself feeling a little embarrassed when I lifted the towels to find a very large wet spot on the crotch of my jeans. *"Geeezus...now I have to change my jeans!"* As I stripped off my pants, I decided to take a quick shower so Roni wouldn't think it was weird that I changed.

In the privacy of the shower stall, I decided to relieve the tension. I closed my eyes and could very clearly recall the curvature of her breasts against that tight sweater. I could envision her gorgeous ass swaying back and forth as we climbed the stairs. I leaned back against the wall and stroked myself very slowly, enjoying every moment of thinking about what it would be like to mount her from behind and fill her with my cock.

"Oh Roni...I want to fuck you," I was thinking her name just as I began to ejaculate.

"I LEFT A ROBE ON THE BACK OF THE DOOR!"

My cock was still spewing as her voice came from just outside the bathroom door. "YOU LEFT YOUR LUGGAGE DOWNSTAIRS," she added.

I stared down at the wad of cum that landed on my foot and wondered if I had SAID her name out loud.

~~oOo~~

I felt a little self-conscious as I went downstairs to grab my luggage. The very nice satin robe that Roni had left for me was very short. Although it fit me properly for the sort of robe it was, I felt like my ass was hanging out as I bent over to get my suitcase.

"Great legs, Casey," she was just behind the counter gawking at me.

"Thanks for the robe!" I gasped as I turned around to go back up the stairs. As I carried both of my bags up the stairs, the belt came loose and the robe fell open. I was very thankful that my back was to Roni as I got to the top of the stairs.

"N-i-i-i-i-c-e Buns!" Roni called up the stairs.

With the robe open in front, it was loose enough in back that she could see my entire ass from where she was standing.

"Like you said...great views!" I referred to our earlier conversation.

The sound of her laughter was like wonderful music as she giggled about my quick reply.

Even though I was red in the face and embarrassed deeply, it made me feel great that she had liked my legs and butt. It also was a hopeful sign that she had not been bashful about saying so. It made me think that perhaps I should be a little freer with my observations of her.

When I finally came back downstairs, (fully dressed now), Roni was in the process of donning her winter parka. "I need to go do some shopping to get ready for this storm that's coming in," she informed me. I was amazed at how truly beautiful she was even in a bulky winter parka.

"Would you like some help?" I offered.

I was pleased when her face completely lit up at my suggestion. "I would love that!" she told me softly. "It will give me a chance to show you the town, too." Her voice sounded like she was genuinely pleased. I put on my ski jacket and we were off.

I felt happy when she reached down and held my hand as we walked across the parking lot at the Super Duper Mart.

"We can get everything we will need right here," she advised as we walked into the store.

I noticed several heads turning as we walked down the aisles, selecting the items that we might need.

"Small town!" Roni chuckled when she saw that I was watching all the glances and nosey whispers. "It's been a long time since they have seen me with a man." She smiled up at me as she said it.

"Oh? Are you usually with women?" I teased her.

I again got to hear her wonderfully musical laughter as she guffawed about my witty reply. "I was right about you, Casey," she squeezed my hand as she said it. "You are going to be so fun." She bent her head up and kissed me on the cheek right there in front of all the gawking people. "Now they'll really have something to gossip about," she laughed.

"I hope we have at least half the fun that they will be gossiping about."

As she again laughed, I squeezed her hand. I had not meant that as a joke but was glad to hear her happiness. "We'll just have to try our best," I added softly.

Her eyes were still smiling as she answered me. "Yes, we will!" She squeezed my hand back.

We made our way through the store and purchased things that would be needed if we lost power or got stranded by heavy snow falls and road closures. Batteries and candles headed the list. Cases of water and canned goods that could be consumed without cooking were next. Roni also made it a point to buy some "goodies" that included two bottles of brandy.

She again held my hand as we made our way back to her SUV after paying for our goods. I noticed that she had opened her parka when we got into the vehicle. I could also see that her nipples were very hard against her tight sweater as she leaned forward to start the vehicle.

"That was fun!" she said cheerfully. "That was the most fun I had shopping in a long time," she added.

As we drove back towards her home, I got to see some of the damage from the hill slide that I was here to survey and calculate damages for. There were a dozen homes on the west end of town completely buried under snow, and a dozen more partially buried. The entire west end of town was blocked by snow and all roads closed. Several businesses were also either destroyed or damaged heavily.

"Looks like I'll be here quite a while," I said it as a matter of fact.

Roni reached over and sat her right hand on my thigh. "I'd like that, Casey," she whispered. "You are welcome for as long as it takes." It felt like she lightly brushed her fingers up and down my thigh before she pulled her hand back. "I'll be happy to have you," she added.

I was fighting the urge to reach over and fondle her all the way back. And fighting the woody that was trying to rise in my jeans. I was grateful that there were bags to carry in when we arrived.

It was already getting dark when we got back so Roni asked me to build a fire in the living room fireplace while she cooked dinner. I had not noticed that she also ran upstairs to get changed while I was busy doing my task.

"Dinner's ready!" She called from the kitchen.

I practically stopped in my tracks when I walked in and saw her.

Roni had taken off her sweater and was now wearing a thin white camisole type top that ended just above her belly button. It was very tight and conformed very erotically to every curve of her luscious breasts. Although it wasn't transparent, it was thin enough that I could just barely see her nipples through the fabric.

"My God, you're gorgeous!" I was surprised that I had said the words out loud. But as she turned and smiled at me, I was glad that I had. She was also now wearing a very short pair of cut-off jean shorts, like those "Daisy Duke" types. Her shapely, powder white legs looked wonderful as she slowly walked towards me.

"Glad you approve," she answered me softly.

We chatted light heartedly throughout dinner. The entire time I had a raging prick that was throbbing painfully in my jeans. My mind racing with images of Roni's voluptuous body, and many lurid images of the sexual things I would like to do with her. We were putting our dishes into the sink when I decided to take a leap.

I moved behind her and kissed the back of her neck.

"Please tell me that you are as attracted as I am feeling for you," I whispered in her ear. I moved my hands up her front and gently cupped her breasts in both hands. There was a momentary pause and I was dreading that I had gone too far. I was about to let go of her breasts when I felt her press back against my body.

"Yessss, Casey," she whispered. I could feel her body trembling. "I feel that too." She was turning into my arms just as the lights went out. We were in total darkness except for a slight glow coming from the fireplace in the living room. She craned her neck up and began to kiss me…

If you enjoyed this sample then look for **The Inn Keeper's Wizard.**

Also by this Author:

About the Author

Jack Ryder LOVES everything there is about sex!

When he is not involved with his "swinger" friends, enjoying a steamy threesome, or being part of a raunchy "gang bang", you can find him on first class planes, trains, and cruise ships. Traveling seems to be the BEST way to finding new and interesting sexmates for him. Sexmates. Plural. He lives with the saying "The More, The Merrier!"

He owns a successful business in New York. He writes as a hobby and also as sort of documentation of his mind-blowing sexcapades over the years. He is presently roaming around the streets of Manhattan but can be anywhere in the world too, since he travels often. So, beware! You just might be his next mate.

*"The most fun thing I enjoy when writing my stories is trying to figure out which is fantasy and which was memory. ENJOY! (Preferably with a friend. *wink*)" -Jack Ryder-*

From the Author

If you have any comments, suggestions, or would just like to get a little personal, please feel free to email me at:
jack_ryder@awesomeauthors.org

If you enjoyed any of my books then please share the love and click like on my books in Amazon.

If you write me a review and send me an email I will send you a free book, or many.
(Just know that these emails are filtered by my publisher.)

Good news is always welcome.

One Last Thing, For Kindle Readers...

When you turn the page, Kindle will give you the opportunity to rate this book and share your thoughts on Facebook and Twitter. If you enjoyed my writings, would you please take a few seconds to let your friends know about it? Because... when they enjoy they will be grateful to you and so will I.

Thank You!

Jack Ryder
jack_ryder@awesomeauthors.org